Look out! It's the Wolf!

Emile Jadoul

In a house on the hill
lived Mr Deer.
Mr Deer was keeping
watch at his window.

Rabbit was
running up
to the house.

"Let me in, Mr
Deer. The wolf
is coming."

"Come in, Rabbit,
and keep watch
with me."

Mr Deer and
Rabbit looked out
of the window.

"Mr Deer... Rabbit... Let me in!" squeaked Pig. "The wolf is coming."

"Come in quickly, Pig,
and keep watch with us."

Mr Deer,
Rabbit
and Pig
looked out
of the
window.

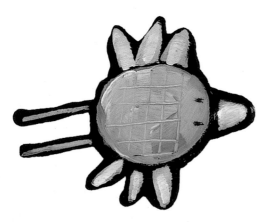

"Mr Deer... Rabbit... Pig,
Let me in!" cried Bear.
"The wolf is coming."

"Come in quickly, Bear,
and keep watch with us."

"Look out!" cried Mr Deer.
"Look out!" cried Rabbit.
"Look out!" cried Pig.
"Look out!" cried Bear.
"Here comes the wolf!"
they all cried.

"Happy birthday,
Mr Wolf!"